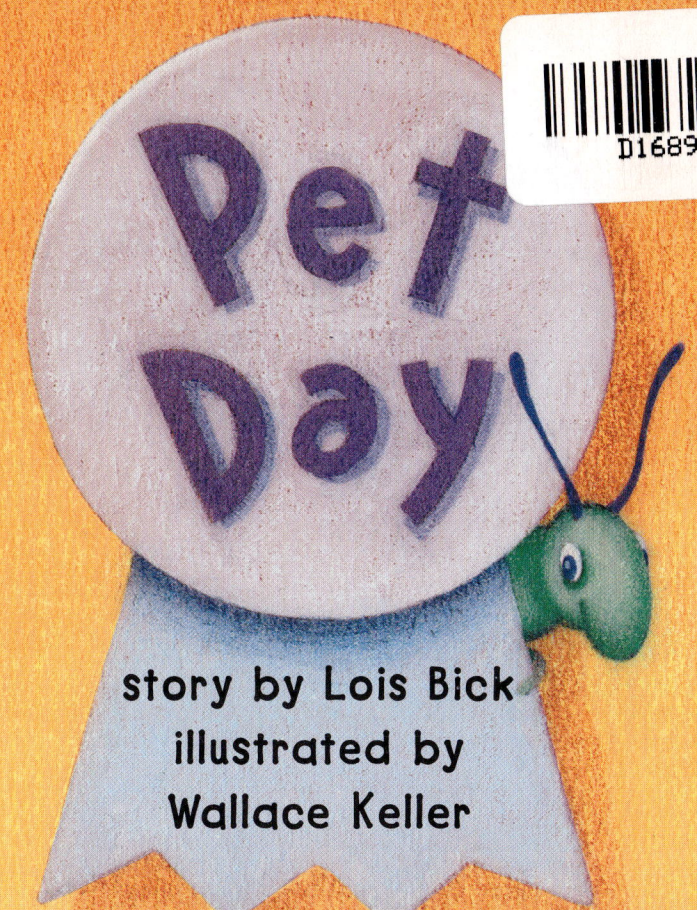

Pet Day

story by Lois Bick
illustrated by Wallace Keller

HARCOURT BRACE & COMPANY

Orlando Atlanta Austin Boston San Francisco Chicago Dallas New York
Toronto London

On Pet Day, all the kids take their pets to school.

Every pet wins a prize.

Last year on Pet Day, Jerome's dog won a prize. The dog is very big.

Marcy's snake won a prize.
The snake is very long.

This year I had an idea. I went outside by the front steps, and I started to hunt.

Then I found something special to take to school. I knew that my pets would win a prize this year.

Jerome brought his mouse.
He chased it most of the day.

Marcy carried her guinea pig.
She let everyone hold it.

Juan held his turtle.
He couldn't get it to
come out of its shell.

Cassie walked in with her monkey.
She trained it to do tricks.

And do you know what?
My pets won a prize, too.

And everyone loved catching my grasshoppers.